P9-BIE-915

Raising
URSA

Nicole S. Amato and Carol A. Amato
Illustrated by David Wenzel

BARRON'S

Anderson

Dedication
This book is dedicated to Connie.

All inquiries should be addressed to:
Barron's Educational Series, Inc.
250 Wireless Boulevard
Hauppauge, New York 11788

International Standard Book No. 0-8120-9310-0

Library of Congress Catalog Card No. 95-36475
Library of Congress Cataloging-in-Publication Data

Amato, Carol A.
    Raising Ursa / Carol A. Amato and Nicole S. Amato; illustrated by
David Wenzel.
        p. cm.—(Young readers' series)
    Summary: Based on the true story of a sea lion pup born in an
aquarium, found to have a broken jaw and an infection, and nursed
to recovery by her keepers.
    ISBN 0-8120-9310-0
    1. California sea lion—Massachusetts—Brewster—Biography—
Juvenile literature. 2. California sea lion—Juvenile literature.
3. Cape Cod Aquarium. [1. California sea lion. 2. Sea lions.]
I. Amato, Nicole S. II. Wenzel, David, 1950–   ill. III. Title.
IV. Series: Amato, Carol A. Young readers' series.
SF408.6.S32A46 1996
636'.9746—dc20   95-36475
                                                      CIP
                                                      AC

PRINTED IN HONG KONG
5678 9955 987654321

Table of Contents

A Pup Is Born

Chapter 1

On an early June day, a young California sea lion gives birth to her first pup. The pup is born at an aquarium on the East Coast in Massachusetts. She is found in the aquarium's sea lion habitat, or living space, by the marine mammal keepers.

They are very excited! The pup is already nursing her mother's warm milk. Her mother's name is Chili Pepper, and her father's name is Sultan.

A Pup Is Born

On an early June day, a young California sea lion gives birth to her first pup. The pup is born at an aquarium on the East Coast in Massachusetts. She is found in the aquarium's sea lion habitat, or living space, by the marine mammal keepers.

They are very excited! The pup is already nursing her mother's warm milk. Her mother's name is Chili Pepper, and her father's name is Sultan.

Chili is a three-year-old member of this sea lion colony or group. Sultan is the father of all the pups here. Like all male sea lions, he will breed with several females. After the pups are born, the father sea lion does not pay attention to them. He is not being mean.

This is the way male sea lions were meant to behave. The males are much larger than females and can reach 600 to 800 pounds (272 to 363 kilograms). Sultan's loud bark can be heard all around the aquarium grounds!

All of the seals and sea lions were either rescued or born at the aquarium. Chili was born here and Sultan was rescued. Many of the animals cannot be returned to the wild. They still need special care. One of the harbor seals is blind and would not be able to live on her own.

In the wild, the sea lion colony may be very large. At this aquarium, the colony is small, with only seven sea lions. They share the pools with four harbor seals. They

are able to do this because they are both members of
the family of marine mammals called pinnipeds.
Pinnipeds include other kinds of sea lions and seals
and walruses. They live all over the world. California
sea lions in the wild live on the Pacific coast of
California.

Just as the new pups are born this time of year at the aquarium, wild California sea lions give birth in late May and early June.

In the wild during the breeding season, sea lions live together in large, crowded groups called rookeries. The sea lions breed and raise their young here. It can become very dangerous for the sea lion pups that are tiny and depend on their mothers for protection. Only the strongest pups will live.

Here at the aquarium, Chili and her pup live with many other animals in their pools. It is a somewhat crowded rookery since the pools are small. Chili must be as careful and protective as a wild sea lion mother would be in a natural rookery.

The pup's first days of life will be spent learning many important things. Chili must be a very good teacher.

Chili and her newborn pup will learn each other's call and smell. Each sea lion mother and her pup have their own special call, which is unlike those of other sea lions. This is the special way they communicate, or send messages, to one another.

In the wild it is very easy for the young pup to get
lost in the crowded rookery. Here at the aquarium,
a mother and pup may become separated, too. If this
happens, the mother and pup call out to each other
with a special bark. Once together, the mother uses
her good sense of smell to tell her pup from the others.

Like all sea lions, this mother will care for her pup
from six months to one year. When the pup is strong
enough to take care of itself, it will learn to fish on its
own. For the months to come, Chili and her pup will
be together all of the time.

Sea lions spend much of their day lying in the sun.
They do this to warm up. When they are resting on
land, they look like happy, lazy sunbathers!

The pup stays by Chili's side at all times and nurses often, both night and day. A mother sea lion's milk is rich in fat and protein. Protein is needed by animals to grow. The sea lion needs a layer of fat under its skin to help it keep warm. This fat is called blubber. The pups are born with a thick coat of fur that also helps to keep them warm.

Chili must also protect her new pup. The sea lions and seals are very curious and try to get close to the pup. Chili watches the keepers carefully when they come into her area. She does not let other pinnipeds and people get too close.

It's feeding time at the aquarium. Chili leaves the pup for a minute to get her fill of fish. The pup stays where Chili has left her, lying in the June sun. Now and then she tries to follow Chili. The pup is very clumsy right now, and the keepers laugh as they watch her.

Sea lions spend much of their lives in the water. They spend hours fishing, surfing on waves, and chasing everything that moves. They are very playful!

Sea lion pups are not ready to swim right away. Chili must help the pup get used to the water. One day, the pup lies a little too close to the edge of the pool and hits the water with a loud splash. She looks so surprised! She is not quite ready to swim yet and looks happy when she gets back on land.

Sea lions use their large front flippers to push
themselves through the water. Their long, smooth
bodies allow the water to glide easily over them.
Because of this, they can reach speeds of up to 15 miles
per hour. That's three times faster than the fastest
Olympic swimmers. Twisting and turning in the water
also helps them move quickly to swim and catch fish.
In time, the pups learn to do the same.

Chapter 4

Ursa Minor

The sea lion keepers pay very close attention to Chili and her new pup. They observe, or watch, the sea lions' feeding habits. They observe how lively they are and how they behave with the other animals.

The sea lions are trained so that the keepers can examine them every day. This is important to keep these beautiful animals healthy and happy.

It is time for Chili's pup to be examined by the animal doctor, or veterinarian. Much to the keepers' surprise, Chili allows them to take her pup to be examined. The keepers will also weigh and measure her every day. They must make sure the pup is growing as a healthy sea lion should. Chili is a very young mother, so the keepers must be sure Chili can care well for her baby.

The veterinarian feels that the pup is small for her age. She is not lively and often seems weak. They will all watch her very carefully in the days to come.

After some time, the keepers decide they must name the pup. She has become the star of the aquarium! People come from all around to see her and want to know her name. The keepers think hard for many days. They decide that they will name her after the constellation Ursa Minor, or Little Bear. Because sea lions are thought to be descendants of bears *and* because this pup is quite a star now, it seems a fitting name! So, Ursa it will be.

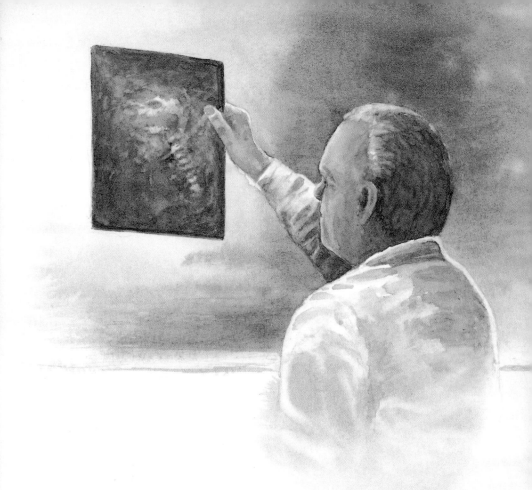

After three weeks, young Ursa is still small and weak. She has not gained much weight and often does not nurse. The keepers are very worried. They call the vet, who comes quickly. Ursa is given an X ray, to look inside her body, and many tests to try to find what is wrong. The keepers are sad to learn that Ursa has a broken jaw. She also has an infection that is much like a person's cold.

They are afraid Chili is not able to give Ursa the care she needs. Something must be done at once. Ursa is placed in a small carrier. She sleeps quietly while the keepers prepare an infant seal formula. This mixture is very much like her mother's warm healthy milk but as thick as a milk shake! They all hope the formula will help her grow strong.

The keepers must get food into her tiny belly at once. There is not enough time to train her to drink from a baby bottle, which is not like nursing from her mother.

The veterinarian knows of another way to feed Ursa. A tube is placed into her mouth. It is carefully pushed down until it reaches her stomach. The tube bends easily, and it will not hurt Ursa. The keepers pour the warm, rich formula into the tube. In minutes, Ursa's belly is full, and she is returned to her mother for a nap in the sun.

The keepers begin to feel more hopeful about Ursa now. Each day, they remove her from the pool to be fed and examined. Chili does not like Ursa to be away from her for long. She calls after her and waits for her return at the entrance of the sea lion habitat.

Ursa is given medicine for her infection. The veterinarian puts a small sturdy wire in her jaw to help it heal. This does not seem to bother Ursa, who has become quite used to all this special attention!

After a week, Ursa is much stronger. The infection is going away and her jaw is healing, but there is a new problem. Ursa is much bigger now and can move much faster than before. She has become very hard to catch. Sea lions can run very fast by moving all four of their flippers. Ursa always wins these chase races, and although the keepers are glad she is so full of energy, they are now the tired ones! The veterinarian and the keepers decide they must find a better way to care for Ursa.

A pool within a pen is built just for her. It is made out of sturdy materials so that it will be a safe place for the young sea lion. It is placed near the big sea lion pools and it is filled with all kinds of playthings. It is sad that Ursa cannot be with her mother and the other sea lions. But she must live this way for now so that she can continue becoming healthy and strong.

Chapter 6

Caring for Ursa

Each keeper must be like a mother to Ursa. Raising a baby is not an easy task. Ursa needs as much attention as a human baby. She is fed six times a day. She is given toys and is often free to roam as she pleases around the food preparation room. Every room must be kept extra clean. She has become very curious and playful. Her favorite toy is a yellow plastic bat. She guards it carefully!

Ursa becomes quite used to the people around her. When she is left in her pen, she often calls out to Chili. Chili recognizes her special call and calls right back. At least mother and pup know that they are not far apart.

Sea lions are not pets like cats and dogs. The keepers must take special care to be sure that Ursa will keep her sea lion ways. If they did not do this, she might "imprint" on one of her keepers. In most animals, imprinting happens soon after the young are born. During this time, the mother and baby learn to know one another. There is a special bond between them. This is very important to the sea lion mother and pup, who must stick together in the crowded rookeries.

Sometimes baby animals raised by humans think that they are humans or that humans are their animal parents. Later on, they may have problems living with other animals or working with other keepers. The keepers must be very careful that this doesn't happen.

When an animal stops drinking its mother's milk, it is ready to be weaned, or trained to eat solid food. The keepers hope Ursa may be ready to learn to fish because she is so hard to catch and tube feed.

They try many ways to get Ursa interested in fish. They put small live fish into her pool. Ursa chases after them, catching them in her mouth and tossing them into the air. To Ursa, fish are not something to eat but are great toys!

In the sea, a pinniped pup would learn to eat fish by watching its mother and the other sea lions feed. In the aquarium, pups watch the others take fish from the keepers' hands. But Ursa sees only humans now, who don't eat like sea lions.

At Ursa's next feeding, instead of tube feeding her, the keepers put a small fish into her mouth. What's this? Ursa looks so surprised! She does not like this at all and chews the fish into many pieces without eating it. She doesn't understand that she must swallow a fish whole. Sea lions don't chew their food. After many tries and many days, at last, she swallows the fish. Hooray! Ursa has "caught" her first meal.

In the days that follow, Ursa learns to eat whole fish without the help of the keepers. She is given small fish which includes herring, smelt, capelin, and squid. All of these are food that seals and sea lions eat in the wild. Each day, she is beginning to look and act more like a healthy sea lion.

This seems like the perfect time to let Ursa return to her mother and the other sea lions for a short visit. The keepers carry her into the pool. The pup is careful at first, but then bounds into the pool area. Soon she sees the water and jumps right in! She has become a great swimmer and diver.

The other animals are curious and come up to smell her. The keepers want to see if Chili will greet her pup. The two had stopped calling to one another weeks ago. In the wild, after a pup stops nursing, it will leave its mother to learn how to fish and live on its own. Scientists are not sure if a mother sea lion and her pup spend time together once the pup can feed itself. Chili no longer acts motherly to Ursa, but she may still know her pup. Sea lions and people do not behave in the same ways.

The keepers are very happy that Ursa has done so well. They will never forget their time caring for her. It has been an exciting time for everyone. The keepers know how important it is to take good care of all the animals living at the aquarium. The animals here are not pets and need a different kind of care and attention than animals that live at home. Raising Ursa taught the keepers many important things about caring for a young sea lion. It also gave the aquarium visitors the chance to learn about this special sea lion and others like her.

Animals are kept in zoos and aquariums for a very important reason: The more we see and learn about other living things, the more likely we are to love, respect, and conserve their rightful place in the wilds of the world.

Afterword

Raising Ursa is based on a true story. The young sea lion was born in June, 1992 at Cape Cod Aquarium/Atlantic Education Center in Brewster, Massachusetts. The aquarium closed in September of that same year.

The success of Ursa's recovery was due to the care and work of many people: the marine mammal care staff and volunteers of Cape Cod Aquarium and New England Aquarium of Boston, Massachusetts, particularly the New England Aquarium's animal care center and marine mammal training staff. Their hard work, supervision, and knowledge helped greatly to ensure her successful recovery. Ursa and her mother, the other sea lions, harbor seals, and other marine animals living there were moved to other aquariums, both in this country and abroad, under the supervision and care of the marine mammal staff of New England Aquarium. Chili is presently living in an aquarium in Florida and Ursa lives in an aquarium in England.

Although it may seem sad that Ursa and Chili were separated, we know that in their natural habitat of the sea, they would also have gone their own wild ways. It is the people who will remember and miss them!

Glossary

bark some animals bark to send messages (communicate). Barking animals include members of the canine (dog) family and the pinnipeds (seals and sea lions).

behave (be-HAVE) behave is the way in which a living thing acts. Animal trainers often teach or train animals behaviors that they might not do in the wild. They often use hand signals or whistles when they train them. The animals may be rewarded with a bit of food. It often takes a long time to train an animal to perform just one behavior.

bond when people or animals develop a special feeling or tie to one another, it is called bonding. Bonding usually takes place soon after an animal is born. A young animal will often bond with the first animal or person that cares for it, even if this is not its birth parent.

breeding season (BREED-ing SEA-son) animals mate in the time of year, or breeding season, according to their kind (species). For example, the pupping season for California sea lions is mid-May to late June. The mother sea lion carries her pup for about 11 months before it is born.

California sea lion (Cal-i-FORN-i-a) people often see California sea lions in zoos, aquariums, and circuses. They are trained easily and become excellent performers. In the wild, California sea lions live along the Pacific coast of California. In autumn and winter, rookeries range as far north as the northern tip of Vancouver Island. California sea lions belong to a group called the eared seals. (See also seal).

colony (COL-o-ny) a colony is a group of living things of the same kind (species) that live together. Sea lion colonies help these animals to survive. They can huddle together in cold weather. They offer protection from predators because there is often safety in numbers.

constellation (con-stell-A-tion) scientists who studied the sky (astronomers) of long ago divided the sky into star patterns, or constellations. We still use these "sky maps" today. The constellations are named after well-known figures and animals. In total, 88 constellations cover the sky.

descendant (de-SCEN-dant) living things' descendants are those that lived before they were born. People's descendants are ancestors (AN-ces-tors) or those in their family who came before them.

harbor seal (HAR-bor seal) harbor seals are the true or earless seals. True seals can hear but their ears cannot be seen. On land, harbor seals wriggle on their bellies and pull themselves along. They grow to be 5 to 6 feet (1.5 to 1.8 meters) long. They are called harbor seals because they often appear in the harbors of cities and towns.

infant seal formula (IN-fant seal FORM-u-la) an infant seal formula is similar to an infant human formula because both have a form of milk and vitamins and minerals. However, only the seal formula has fish!

marine mammals (mar-INE MAMM-als) marine
mammals are animals that live mostly in the sea or
rivers. They live anywhere from tropical waters to
the North and South poles. Like land mammals,
they are warm-blooded (their temperature stays
about the same all the time); they breathe air
through their lungs; they give birth to live young;
they nurse their young (drink milk from their
mother's bodies); and they have hair or fur at
some time in their development.
The marine mammals include:

1) whales (including dolphins and porpoises)
2) seals, sea lions, walruses
3) manatees, dugongs, sea cows
4) polar bears, sea otters

nurse mammal mothers nurse their young with
mammary glands in the belly area. A healthy mother's
milk is a thin liquid full of complete nourishment for
her young. It is all they need until they are weaned
and ready to eat solid food.

pinnipeds (PINN-i-peds) the word pinniped means
fin- or feather-footed. Pinnipeds are mammals whose
habitat is the water. The pinnipeds include the true
or earless seals, the eared seals, and the walruses.
They live all over the world, from the frozen north to
warm, tropical waters.

rookery (ROOK-er-y) a rookery is the breeding ground
for certain birds and mammals that live together in
groups. California sea lion males (bulls) mate with
several females, many of whom will give birth to
their young. The bulls defend small parts of beach

that may be near reefs, rocks, or tide pools where the females will raise and nurse the pups.

seal earless seals are members of the pinniped family. They are called the true seals. This group includes the monk seal, elephant seal, hooded seal, gray seal, harbor seal, and many others. True seals and eared seals have many differences. One of these differences can be seen in the way they move. True seals move by dragging themselves on land on their bellies. Eared seals can move on land by using their front and back flippers.

weaning (WEAN-ing) weaning takes place when a mother (human or animal) decides that it is time for her young to stop nursing. The mother then tries to interest the young in more solid food. In the wild, sea lion pups are weaned at about six months old.

Dear Parents and Educators:

Welcome to the Young Readers' series!

These learning stories have been created to introduce young children to the study of animals.

Children's earliest exposure to reading is usually through fiction. Stories read aloud invite children into the world of words and imagination. If children are read to frequently, this becomes a highly anticipated form of entertainment. Often that same pleasure is felt when children learn to read on their own. Nonfiction books are also read aloud to children but generally when they are older. However, interest in the "real" world emerges early in life, as soon as children develop a sense of wonder about everything around them.

There are a number of excellent read-aloud natural-science books available. Educators and parents agree that children love nonfiction books about animals. Unfortunately, there are very few that can be read *by* young children. One of the goals of the Young Readers' series is to happily fill that gap!

Raising Ursa is one in a series of learning stories designed to appeal to young readers. In the classroom, the series can be incorporated into literature-based or whole-language programs, and would be especially suitable for science theme teaching units. Within planned units, each book may serve as a springboard to immersion techniques that include hands-on activities, field study trips, and additional research and reading. Many of the books are also concerned with the threatened or endangered status of the species studied and the role even young people can play in the preservation plan.

These books can also serve as read-aloud for young children. Weaving information through a story form lends itself easily to reading aloud. Hopefully, this book and others in the series will provide entertainment and wonder for both young readers and listeners.

C.A.

In the Classroom

One of the goals of this series is to introduce the young child to factual information related to the species being studied. The science terminology used is relevant to the learning process for the young student. In the classroom, you may want to use multi-modality methods to ensure understanding and word recognition. The following suggestions may be helpful:

1. Refer to the pictures when possible for difficult words and discuss how these words can be used in another context.

2. Encourage the children to use word and sentence contextual clues when approaching unknown words. They should be encouraged to use the glossary since it is an important information adjunct to the story.

3. After the children read the story or individual chapter, you may want to involve them in discussions using a variety of questioning techniques:

   a. Questions requiring *recall* ask the children about past experiences, observations, or feelings. (*Have you ever seen movies or TV programs about sea lions?*)

   b. *Process* questions help the children to discover relationships by asking them to compare, classify, infer, or explain. (*Do you have to eat every day? Does the sea lion? Why or why not?*)

   c. *Application* questions ask children to use new information in a hypothetical situation by evaluating, imagining, or predicting.

At Home

The above aids can be used if your child is reading independently or aloud. Children will also enjoy hearing this story read aloud to them. You may want to use some of the questioning suggestions above. The story may provoke many questions from your child. Stop and answer the questions. Replying with an honest, "I don't know," provides a wonderful opportunity to head for the library to do some research together!

Have a wonderful time in your shared quest of discovery learning!

Carol A. Amato
Language-Learning Specialist